The Miller and His Sons

The Donkey in the Lion's Skin

Illustrated by Val Biro

Award Publications Limited

An old farmer had worked hard all his life. He grew big, juicy grapes in his vineyard.

People paid a lot of money for his grapes, but the farmer was not happy. He was worried.

The farmer had three sons. They were very lazy and never did any work on the vineyard.

He worried that they would not take good care of the vineyard after he died.

The farmer knew that his sons did not understand the importance of hard work.

One day he had an idea. He told them, "When I am gone, remember that there is a great treasure in my vineyard."

When the farmer died, his sons remembered what he had said. Thoughts of gold, bags of coins, and chests of silver filled their heads.

"We will dig for the treasure!" they cried. They ran to the vineyard with a shovel, a fork and a hoe and set to work.

They dug out every weed to look for pearls underneath. They turned over the hard soil to look for silver coins.

Week after week, the sons worked hard in the vineyard, but they did not find a single penny or nugget of gold.

When they had worked
over the last piece of soil they
stopped. "Father must have
played a trick on us," they said.

Tired from their hard work, the sons fell asleep. They were very disappointed that they had not found any treasure.

But they had dug the vineyard so well that the grapes grew bigger than ever before! When the grapes were ripe, the sons took them to market.

Everybody wanted to buy some of the marvellous grapes. Soon the sons' pockets were full of money.

"The grapes are the treasure in the vineyard!" the sons cried. "If we work hard there will be more treasure next harvest."

The farmer's sons now knew the importance of hard work.

The Donkey in the Lion's Skin

One day a donkey found a
lion's skin lying on the ground.
He sniffed it to make sure there
was not a lion still inside it.
Then he had an idea.

"I am not a brave donkey, but perhaps if people believe I am a lion they will think I am strong!" He put on the skin like a coat.

The donkey trotted down into
the village square. The people
could not believe their eyes.
"Help! It is a lion!" they wailed.

The donkey
thought what fun it was when
everyone ran away in fright.

The donkey chased after them, but as he ran the lion's skin slipped off his back.

He tried to roar, but all that came out was: "HEE-HAW!"

The villagers saw he was not a lion after all. "We are not afraid of a donkey!" they cried.

They were angry that the donkey had tricked them.

Without the lion's skin, the donkey no longer felt brave. So he ran away as fast as his legs would carry him.